My Secret Unicorn

Dreams Come True

Mel turned Shadow towards the jump.
His ears pricked up and he quickened his
stride. 'He's going to jump it!' Lauren
whispered to Twilight in delight.
Shadow got nearer and nearer, his
hooves thudding on the grass.
Then, a metre in front of the jump,
he suddenly stopped.

My Secret Unicorn

Dreams Come True

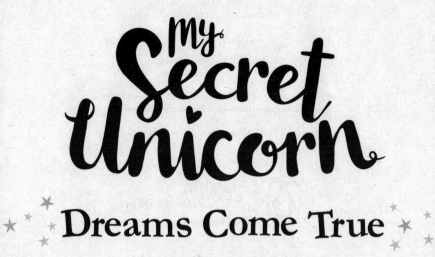

Linda Chapman

Illustrated by Biz Hull

PUFFIN

PUFFIN BOOKS

UK | USA | Canada | Ireland | Australia
India | New Zealand | South Africa

Puffin Books is part of the Penguin Random House group of companies
whose addresses can be found at global.penguinrandomhouse.com.

www.penguin.co.uk   www.puffin.co.uk   www.ladybird.co.uk

Penguin
Random House
UK

First published 2002
This edition published 2018

005

Written by Linda Chapman
Text copyright © Working Partners Ltd, 2002
Illustrations copyright © Biz Hull, 2002
Created by Working Partners Ltd, London W6 0QT

The moral right of the author and illustrator has been asserted

Typeset in 14.25/21.5 pt Bembo
Printed in Great Britain by Clays Ltd, Elcograf S.p.A.

A CIP catalogue record for this book is available from the British Library

ISBN: 978-0-241-36917-3

All correspondence to:
Puffin Books
Penguin Random House Children's
80 Strand, London WC2R ORL

*To Iola – dreams really
can come true*

One

'It's almost time, Twilight,' Lauren Foster whispered to the grey pony beside her. She looked down at the star-shaped flower in her hand. At the tip of each purple petal, a golden spot glowed. The pony stamped one of his front hooves and pushed at her hand impatiently.

'Just a few more minutes,' Lauren told

him. She looked up. The sun had almost
set. This was the moment she'd been
waiting for all day. As the last of the sun
disappeared behind the mountains, a
bright star shone out overhead.

A thrill ran through Lauren. *Now!*

Gently, she began to crumble the petals of the flower between her fingers. As she did so, she whispered the secret words of the Turning Spell.

Twilight Star, Twilight Star,
Twinkling high above so far.
Shining light, shining bright,
Will you grant my wish tonight?
Let my little horse forlorn
Be at last a unicorn!

Almost before the last word had left Lauren's mouth, there was a bright purple flash.

The patch of grass where Twilight had been standing was empty. Lauren looked up. A snow-white unicorn was cantering in circles in the sky.

'Twilight!' Lauren exclaimed in delight.

With a kick of his back legs, Twilight swooped down and landed beside Lauren.

'Hello,' he said, putting his nose close to hers and blowing out softly. Although Twilight's words rang out clearly in Lauren's head, his mouth didn't move. Lauren remembered what he had told her when she had first turned him into a unicorn the night before – as long as she was touching him, or holding a hair from his mane, she would be able to hear him speaking.

Lauren hugged him and then looked down at the petals still clutched in her hand. 'But I didn't throw them on the ground,' she said.

Twilight tossed his flowing silver mane. 'You don't need to any more. The moonflower petals are only needed the *first* time the spell is said. You don't even need the light of the Twilight Star. From now on, all you need to do is say the magic words.' He pawed the grass. 'Come on, Lauren. Let's go flying.'

Lauren didn't need to be asked twice. In a flash, she had scrambled on to his back.

Twilight plunged upwards and Lauren laughed in delight as the wind whipped through her hair. She held on to Twilight's long mane.

'I'm getting better at flying,' Twilight said, cantering in a smooth circle.

'Definitely!' Lauren agreed.

The day before, Twilight's flying had been quite wobbly and she'd been very glad that special unicorn magic had stopped her from falling off! Now she looked down at the fields and woods below.

'Let's fly over the woods,' Twilight said.

'And jump over the treetops.'

'OK,' Lauren agreed. 'But I can't stay

out too long in case Mum and Dad start wondering where I am.'

Twilight turned in the air and headed for the forest that covered the mountains behind Lauren's house.

Lauren could see the nearby farms spread out beneath them. One in particular caught her attention – a white clapboard farmhouse with red barns that hugged the mountainside at the edge of the forest. 'That's Goose Creek Farm,' she said. 'Dad met the man who owns it today. He's called Mr Cassidy. He's got a daughter called Mel who's the same age as me and she's got a pony. Dad's arranged for me to go and visit them tomorrow and you're coming too!'

'Sounds like fun!' Twilight said.

Lauren suddenly looked anxious. 'What if Mel's pony guesses you're a unicorn?' she said. She knew that it was very important no one discovered Twilight's secret. Lauren had been given the spell to turn Twilight into a unicorn by an old lady called Mrs Fontana, and she had told Lauren that she must never let anyone find out Twilight was a unicorn. It might put him in great danger!

'He'll know,' Twilight said, 'but it'll be OK. Horses and ponies understand that a unicorn's secret must be kept.'

'Do all animals know about unicorns?' Lauren asked curiously.

Twilight shook his head. 'Just horses

and ponies, though sometimes other animals will sense I'm different.' He swooped down so that his hooves were skimming the treetops. 'Now, are you ready to do some jumping?'

'You bet!' Lauren exclaimed.

'Then here goes!' Twilight galloped forward through the air and carried her over the top branches of a tall pine tree.

They leapt from one treetop to the next, giddy with excitement. At the far edge of the forest, Twilight cantered into the air and turned a loop-the-loop. Lauren whooped out loud in delight.

All too soon, Lauren realized it was time to go back home. 'If we're much longer, Mum and Dad might start getting worried,' she said to Twilight.

He nodded and they flew back to
Granger's Farm.

Twilight landed in his paddock. Lauren
dismounted and said the Undoing Spell.
There was a bright purple flash as
Twilight turned from a unicorn into a
small, grey pony.

'See you tomorrow,' Lauren whispered.
She gave him a quick hug, then raced
back to the house.

Her dad was in the kitchen. He
glanced at the kitchen clock. 'You've
been out a long time,' he commented.

'I was just playing with Twilight,'
Lauren said, her heart pounding.

To her relief, her dad smiled. 'I'm glad

you're enjoying having a pony so much,' he said. 'Life here in the country sure beats life back in the city, doesn't it?'

'Totally,' Lauren agreed happily. It was only a week ago that her family had left their house in the city to move to Granger's Farm, so that Mr Foster could follow his dream of becoming a farmer. But already Lauren felt completely at home.

As Lauren passed her brother's bedroom, she heard laughter. She pushed the door open. Her brother, Max, was in bed and Buddy, Max's Bernese mountain dog puppy, was standing on his hind legs with his big white front paws on the covers. His pink tongue was hanging out and he seemed to be trying to lick every inch of Max's face.

'Honestly, Max, I think he'd get into bed with you if I let him!' Mrs Foster exclaimed as she pushed the black and tan puppy down. 'Buddy, you're a pest,' she scolded, but she smiled as she spoke.

Buddy came gambolling over to Lauren. Not managing to stop in time, he skidded into her legs.

'Oof!' Lauren exclaimed. 'Buddy! You weigh a ton!'

'You wait till he's fully grown,' Mrs Foster said with a laugh. 'Now you'd better get ready for bed too, honey. You and Dad are expected at the Cassidys' house at nine-thirty so you're going to

have to be up early to get Twilight fed
and groomed in time.'

Lauren nodded.

'I hope you and Mel Cassidy get
along,' Mrs Foster went on. 'It would be
great for you to have a friend to go
riding with.'

'Yeah,' Lauren agreed. 'I hope Mel's
nice.'

As she went to her bedroom, she
thought about the next day. Would
Mel want to be friends with her? Would
she want to be friends with Mel? She
hoped so.

She got her pyjamas out from under
her pillow and walked to her bedroom
window. She could see the Blue Ridge

Mountains towering up behind the house and, best of all, she could see Twilight's stable and paddock.

'Goodnight, Twilight,' she whispered, looking at the little pony's shadowy shape grazing by the gate. 'I hope tomorrow's going to be OK.'

Twilight looked up. Lauren was sure she saw him whicker. Blowing him a kiss, she smiled and closed the curtain.

CHAPTER

Two

'Buddy! Here, boy!' Max called, crawling under the kitchen table as Lauren ate her cereal the next morning.

Mr Foster was standing by the door talking to Hank and Joe, the two farmhands who helped look after the Fosters' herd of dairy cows and the ten pigs. 'I want to move the calves to the bottom pasture this morning,' Mr Foster was explaining.

Mrs Foster was on the phone. 'Yes, we're finally getting sorted out,' she said, one hand pressed to her ear to shut out the noise in the kitchen.

Lauren got up and put her empty cereal bowl in the dishwasher. 'I'm going to get Twilight ready,' she announced.

The April sun was shining as she stepped outside and the new leaves on the trees looked green and fresh. Lauren breathed in deeply and ran down the path that led from the house to the paddock. Twilight was waiting at the gate. He whinnied when he saw her.

'Hi, fella,' Lauren said, climbing over

the gate. 'I bet you'd like some breakfast.'

Twilight nuzzled her. Snapping the
leadrope on to his head-collar, Lauren led
him up to his stable and fetched him
some pony nuts in a bucket. As he ate,
she looked at her watch. Eight-fifteen.

That meant she had an hour to groom
him before she and her dad had to leave
for the Cassidys' house.

Half an hour later, Lauren stepped back
to admire her handiwork. Twilight's
scruffy grey coat was looking much
cleaner, his hooves gleamed from the
hoof oil and his newly washed tail was
almost dry.

'You look loads better,' Lauren
declared. He whickered in agreement.

'Buddy! Come back!'

Hearing her brother's cry, Lauren
looked round. Buddy was galloping down
the path towards her, his black ears
flopping, his enormous white paws

thudding on the grass. Max tore after
him.

'Buddy! Careful!' Lauren gasped, as the
puppy headed straight for the bucket of
water. Buddy tried to stop but he was too
late. He crashed into it, sending the dirty
suds flying up into the air.

Twilight snorted and jumped back to
the end of his rope, but the contents of
the bucket splashed all over him.

'Buddy!' Lauren exclaimed. She swung
round to Max. He was standing on the
path, his hand fixed to his mouth, his
blue eyes wide with shock. 'Max!' she
cried.

'I'm sorry, I'm really sorry,' Max said. 'I
opened the back door and Buddy just ran

off down the path. I couldn't stop him,
Lauren.'

Lauren sighed. It was no use getting
annoyed with Max. It wasn't his fault that
Buddy was so clumsy. 'It's OK,' she said. 'I
guess I'll just have to groom Twilight again.'

'I'll help you,' Max offered.

Lauren took a towel from the
grooming box and handed it to Max.
'Thanks,' she said.

'Look at Buddy,' Max said suddenly.

Lauren looked at the puppy. He was
crawling on his tummy towards Twilight,
his ears pricked up, his tail wagging like
crazy. 'Woof!' he said, jumping back.
'Woof! Woof!' He sat up and cocked his
head on one side.

'What's he doing?' Max said in surprise.

'I don't know,' Lauren said with a frown. She tried to move the puppy away, but Buddy just kept staring at Twilight. He seemed fascinated. Lauren felt worried. Could Buddy somehow sense that Twilight wasn't a normal pony? She got hold of Buddy's collar again. 'Here, Max. Maybe you should take him back to the house. Twilight might stand on him by mistake if he gets too close.'

'But what about helping you?' Max said, looking disappointed.

'I'll manage,' Lauren replied quickly. She saw Max's mouth open as if to argue. 'We don't want Buddy to get hurt, do we?'

'No,' Max said, taking Buddy's collar.

As he dragged Buddy back to the house, Lauren bit her lip. If Buddy acted like that in front of her mum and dad, they were bound to get suspicious. She looked at Twilight. He was staring after Buddy, and Lauren was sure he looked concerned.

At nine-fifteen, Lauren rode out of Granger's Farm with her father walking beside Twilight. They headed for Goose Creek Farm. It wasn't far and they were soon walking down the drive towards the house. The back door opened and a tall man with black hair came out on to the veranda.

'Mike!' he said, coming forward to greet Mr Foster. 'Hi. And this must be Lauren. Mel can't wait to meet you. She's with Shadow at the moment – that's her pony. Come on, I'll show you round to the paddock.'

Lauren rode after him. As they reached the back of the house, she saw a paddock with two jumps set out. A dapple-grey pony was tethered to the paddock fence. A girl with black curly hair was standing beside him, brushing his shiny coat.

'Mel!' Mr Cassidy called.

The girl turned. Seeing Lauren, her face lit up with a friendly grin. 'Hi!' she called. Throwing her grooming brush down, she jogged over. 'I'm Mel.'

'I'm Lauren,' Lauren said rather shyly.

'Your pony's gorgeous,' Mel said. 'What's he called?'

'Twilight,' said Lauren, dismounting.

'Twilight.' Mel frowned thoughtfully, patting him. 'Did he used to belong to Jade Roberts?'

'That's right,' Lauren said in surprise.

Mel nodded. 'I thought I recognized him. I go to Pony Club with Jade.' She smiled at Lauren. 'My pony's called Shadow. Do you want to come and meet him?'

Lauren nodded eagerly.

'We'll leave you two girls to get to know each other then,' Mr Cassidy said. 'We'll be in the house if you want us.'

Lauren and Mel nodded. 'So, how long have you had Shadow?' Lauren asked, as she led Twilight over to say hello.

'Six months,' Mel replied. 'I couldn't believe it when Mum and Dad bought him for me. I'd wanted a pony for … like forever. I think I was born pony-crazy.'

'Me too!' Lauren agreed, grinning at her.

Shadow turned his head to look at Twilight. Lauren held her breath. What if he acted as strangely as Buddy had?

But, after staring at Twilight for a moment, Shadow simply snorted softly and stretched out his muzzle to say hello.

Twilight blew down his nostrils in reply.

'They like each other!' Mel said. She
beamed at Lauren. 'It's going to be so
cool being neighbours – I can just tell!'
Happiness welled up inside Lauren.

'I'll get Shadow tacked up,' Mel said. 'Then we can play catch in the paddock.'

Lauren and Mel had great fun. Shadow was fast and could turn very quickly, but Twilight was also pretty speedy. They chased each other round the paddock, trying to tag each other, and then they had an egg-and-spoon race, a trotting race and a race where they had to canter around poles stuck in the ground in a line. 'This is loads better than riding on my own!' Mel said as they finished in a dead heat.

'Shall we jump next?' Lauren asked, looking at the fences.

Mel's face fell. 'There's no point,' she

sighed. 'Shadow doesn't jump. I took him
to a Pony Club mounted meeting last
month but he wouldn't even go near a
jump. Watch.'

She cantered Shadow away from
Twilight and turned him towards one of
the fences. He slowed to a trot and then
to a walk. Mel kicked his sides but it
made no difference. He stopped a metre
away from the jump.

'He does it every time,' Mel said,
riding back to Lauren. 'And I don't know
what I'm going to do. There's another
mounted meeting this Saturday and Jade
Roberts and her friend Monica were
really mean about him when he wouldn't
jump last time.'

'Maybe he'll follow Twilight over a jump,' Lauren suggested.

But even when Twilight jumped, Shadow refused to follow. As soon as Mel turned him towards the fences, he slowed down, his ears back.

'It's no use,' Mel sighed. 'He's not going to do it.' She patted Shadow. 'It doesn't matter, Shadow,' she said. 'I love you whether you can jump or not.'

Although Mel tried to smile, Lauren could see the sadness in her new friend's eyes. 'I'll try to think of some other way to help,' Lauren promised. 'If I come over tomorrow after school, maybe we could try again then.'

'That would be great,' Mel said, looking

more cheerful. 'Between the two of us we must be able to think of something.'

They untacked the ponies and turned them out into the paddock to graze. Then Mel showed Lauren around Goose Creek Farm. Just up the track from the barn with Shadow's stall was an enormous red hay-barn. In it was Mel's cat, Sparkle. 'She's just had two kittens,' Mel said to Lauren. 'They're only three weeks old.'

Lauren gasped in delight as she saw the two tiny black kittens snuggled into their mother's side. Sparkle had made a nest in a pile of loose hay at the back of the barn and the two kittens were sleeping beside her.

'What have you called them?' Lauren
asked in a low voice.

'Star and Midnight,' Mel whispered
back. 'Mum and Dad have said I can keep
them both.'

As they walked back down the path
towards the paddock and the farmhouse,
Mel turned to Lauren. 'You know, you
should join Pony Club too. We have
mounted and unmounted meetings every
month, competitions and there's even a
camp in the summer!'

Lauren hesitated, thinking about
the two girls who had been mean to
Mel.

Mel seemed to read her mind. 'It's only
Jade and Monica who are like that,' she

said. 'The others in my group are really nice.'

'OK then,' Lauren agreed. 'I'll ask.'

'You two look like you've been having fun,' Mr Foster said, as Lauren and Mel ran into the large kitchen. He and Mr Cassidy were sitting at the table, having coffee.

'We have!' Lauren exclaimed. 'We went riding and then Mel showed me round, and she wants to know if I can join her Pony Club.' She looked at Mel, who nodded eagerly.

'We could go to the meetings together. It would be cool!' Lauren added. 'Can I join, Dad?'

Mr Foster smiled. 'It sounds like a great idea.'

'I've got the secretary's number somewhere here,' Mr Cassidy said, getting up and rummaging through a pile of papers by the telephone. 'Yes, here we are.' He wrote it down on a piece of paper and handed it to Mr Foster. 'It's a good Pony Club. The kids learn a lot there. There's a mounted meeting next weekend. Lauren and Twilight are very welcome to have a ride there in our trailer.'

'Thanks,' said Mr Foster, taking the paper from him. 'I'll ring the secretary when we get home.'

Lauren and Mel exchanged delighted looks.

'I'm so glad you've moved here,' Mel said, as Lauren got back on Twilight to ride home.

'Me too,' Lauren said, grinning at her.

'Come on, then,' Mr Foster said, patting Twilight's neck. 'Let's go.'

Mel ran along the driveway with them. 'I'll see you at school tomorrow,' she called, as Lauren rode out of the drive.

'So do you like Mel, then?' Mr Foster said to Lauren, as they walked along the road.

'Yeah!' Lauren said. 'She's lots of fun.' She stroked Twilight's neck. She couldn't stop thinking about Shadow's jumping problem. She really wanted to be able to help. But how?

Maybe Twilight will know, she thought.

CHAPTER
Three

After supper, Lauren pulled on her trainers. The sun had just set and she was anxious to get moving. 'I'm just going to check on Twilight,' she said to her mum.

'OK, honey,' Mrs Foster said. 'But don't be out for too long. Remember you've got school starting tomorrow.'

Buddy ran to the door and stood

there, his head cocked on one side.

'You're not coming with me, Buddy,'
Lauren told him. She went outside,
shutting the door carefully behind her,
and hurried down the path to the
paddock. Would Twilight be able to think
of a way to help Shadow?

Twilight whickered when he saw her.
Lauren began to say the words of the
Turning Spell:

Twilight Star, Twilight Star …

Suddenly Twilight whinnied loudly.

Lauren stopped. He seemed to be
staring at something over her shoulder.
She swung round to see what it was.

Buddy was standing on the path
behind her.

'Buddy! Go away!' Lauren exclaimed.
Buddy was curious enough about
Twilight already. If he saw Twilight
change into a unicorn, he would never
leave him alone. She took hold of the
puppy's collar.

'Buddy!' she heard her dad shouting.

'He's here, Dad!' Lauren called back.

Mr Foster came down the path. 'I only
opened the door for a second. Buddy just
raced off after you. Come on, fella,' he
said, taking hold of the puppy's collar.
'You come in with me.'

Lauren waited until she heard the
door of the house shut and then she

whispered the secret words.

There was a purple flash and suddenly Twilight was standing before her, a snow-white unicorn once again.

'That was close,' he said.

'I know,' Lauren said, feeling worried. 'I'm going to have to be so careful. Buddy's far too interested in you.' Suddenly she remembered what she'd been going to ask Twilight. 'Do you know why Shadow won't jump? Mel's really upset about it.'

'I don't know,' Twilight admitted. He pawed the grass. 'But we could visit him and find out.'

'Now?' Lauren said, looking at the sky. It still wasn't properly dark yet. 'But what if Mel or her parents see us?'

'We could go later then,' Twilight said.

Lauren hesitated. 'Well, I guess I could come just after I go to bed,' she said. 'Mum's writing a new book so she'll be working on her computer and Dad's bound to be watching TV. But I won't be able to stay out long.'

'We'll be quick,' Twilight promised.

'All right then,' Lauren agreed. 'I'll come back as soon as I can.' She said the Undoing Spell, turning Twilight back into a pony, and hurried back to the house.

After her mum had said goodnight and gone into her study to work, Lauren pulled her jeans on over her pyjamas and scribbled a quick note for her parents just in case they came to check on her and were worried.

I'll be back soon. I've just gone to see Twilight.
Lots of love, Lauren XXX

Leaving it on her bed, she crept down the stairs and out of the house.

I'll be back as quickly as I can, she told herself as she hurried down to the paddock.

It only took a few seconds to change Twilight into a unicorn. 'Quick!' Lauren said. She scrambled on to his back. 'Let's go!'

They swooped down on Shadow's
paddock at Goose Creek Farm. 'There he
is!' Lauren said, spotting the dark shape of
Mel's dapple-grey pony.

Twilight landed with a
soft whicker just behind
him. Shadow swung
round with an
alarmed
snort.

Twilight whinnied and Lauren saw
Shadow relax. He whinnied back as if he
was talking to Twilight.

'What's he saying?' Lauren asked
Twilight.

'That he knew I was a unicorn,'
Twilight said. 'And he would like to
know why we've come.'

Lauren didn't want to waste any time.
'Ask him why he won't jump,' she said to
Twilight.

'He understands you,' Twilight told her
as Shadow whinnied in reply. Twilight
listened to the dapple-grey pony for a
few moments. 'He's scared,' he told
Lauren. 'He says that when he was a foal,
he was jumping over a tree trunk with

the other foals in his field and he banged
his legs really hard. Ever since then, he's
been afraid of jumping. He hates making
Mel upset but he just can't do it.'

'Have you got any magical powers
that could help him not to feel so scared,
Twilight?' Lauren asked.

'I don't know,' Twilight replied
doubtfully. 'I know I've got some magical
powers, but I'm not sure what they are. I
guess I might be able to help, but I don't
know how.'

Lauren felt disappointed. She'd been
hoping that Twilight would be able to do
some magic and make everything OK.
She thought hard. If they couldn't use
Twilight's powers to help Shadow then

maybe she could come up with a more practical solution. 'If I put the poles from the jumps on the ground do you think you might be able to walk over them?' she asked Shadow.

Shadow snorted.

'He says he might,' Twilight translated.

'Well, that would be a start,' Lauren said. She got off Twilight's back and took two poles and laid them out on the grass. *It's lucky that Shadow's paddock is hidden from the farmhouse,* she thought.

'Try walking over these,' she said to Shadow. 'At least it's a step towards jumping.'

Shadow looked very nervous.

'It'll be OK,' Twilight encouraged him.

Shadow walked up to the first pole and
stopped. Then, snorting loudly, he stepped
over it, picking his hooves up high.

'Well done!' Lauren cried. 'Now try
the other one, Shadow.'

The same thing happened.

'You did it!' Twilight exclaimed as
Shadow trotted back to them, suddenly

looking much happier.

'I'll put up a tiny jump now,' Lauren said. 'Let's see if you can do that.'

But Shadow backed off, whinnying.

Twilight sighed. 'He doesn't want to. He's still too frightened to try a jump.' Shadow neighed. 'If we can come and help him some more, he might get braver.'

It was better than nothing. 'OK, we'll come again tomorrow,' Lauren said. She gave Shadow a hug and then got back on to Twilight. 'We'll help you, Shadow. No matter how long it takes.'

CHAPTER

Four

'Come on, Lauren!' Mrs Foster
called the next morning.

Lauren checked her reflection for the
last time in her bedroom mirror. She was
wearing new jeans and a blue T-shirt. Her
freshly washed hair was tied back in a
ponytail. She swallowed nervously. Her
first day at a new school. What was it
going to be like?

Taking a deep breath, she ran
downstairs. Her mum and Max were
waiting by the door.

'Feeling nervous?' Mrs Foster asked her.

'A little,' Lauren admitted, yawning.

Her mum frowned. 'Didn't you sleep
well last night?'

'I'm fine, Mum,' Lauren said quickly.
She'd got back into the house safely after
her adventure with Twilight and she
didn't want her mum getting suspicious
now. She picked up her school bag.
'Come on. Let's go.'

Silver River Elementary School was only
a ten-minute drive away from Granger's
Farm. It was a low brick building. As

Mrs Foster parked the car, Lauren saw
Mel standing at the school gates. 'There's
Mel!' she exclaimed.

She jumped out of the car and ran
over. 'Hi!'

'Hi!' Mel said. 'I thought I'd wait for
you.'

Mrs Foster and Max walked up to
them. 'This is my mum and my brother,
Max,' Lauren said.

'Pleased to meet you,' Mel said politely.
'I'm in the same class as Lauren, Mrs
Foster. I can show her there if you want.'

Mrs Foster looked questioningly at
Lauren, who nodded. 'Yeah, I'll be fine,
Mum,' she said quickly.

'Well, in that case,' Mrs Foster said,

'that would be a real help, Mel. It gives me more time to get Max settled into his classroom. I'll stop by the office, Lauren, and tell them you're here.'

'Bye, Mum,' said Lauren, giving her a quick kiss. 'I'll see you this afternoon.'

Mrs Foster nodded. 'I'll pick you up here at the gates. Have a good day, honey.'

'She will,' Mel said, swinging her school bag on to her shoulder. 'Come on, Lauren. I want to show you around.'

By morning break, Lauren's nerves had totally disappeared. Mr Noland, her new teacher, was strict but fun. Even better, he'd let her and Mel sit together. The other kids in the class seemed really keen

to be friends too – all apart from Jade
Roberts and her friend Monica Corder.
They hadn't said a word to Lauren or Mel,
although they had giggled when Jade had
leaned over Mel's desk and caught sight of
a horse that Mel had drawn.

'Looks more like a pig than a horse,'
Jade had said to Monica.

'Or a mule,' Monica had said, flicking
her blonde hair back.

'Just like her dumb pony,' Jade went on,
her green eyes looking mockingly at Mel.
'I mean, imagine having a dumb pony that
won't jump. How sad can you get?'

'He's not dumb!' Lauren said angrily.

Jade turned her full attention to her.
'And what do *you* know about horses?'

'Well, I've got one,' Lauren said.

'Lauren Foster?' Jade said suddenly. 'You're the girl who owns Twilight, aren't you?' When Lauren nodded, Jade laughed. 'How sad. I got my dad to sell him because he wasn't good enough to win ribbons. My new pony, Prince, is a hundred times better.'

Lauren glared at them but, before she could say anything, Mr Noland heard the whispering and told Jade and Monica to be quiet.

Lauren was still fuming when the lesson came to an end.

'Come on, Lauren!' Mel said as they went outside. 'Let's go and sit under the tree. I've brought some photos of

Shadow to show you.'

'You know, I had an idea last night,' Lauren said quickly, wanting to cheer her up. 'I think Shadow might be scared of jumping . . . for some reason. We could try walking him over poles on the ground, then, as he gets braver, we could put up some tiny jumps.'

Mel looked doubtful. 'Do you really think it will work?'

'I'm sure,' Lauren said. 'Look, why don't I come over after school with Twilight and we can try then?'

Her enthusiasm seemed to encourage Mel.

'OK,' she said eagerly. 'Let's do it.'

CHAPTER

Five

'Should I try now?' Mel said to
Lauren later that afternoon. She
was mounted on Shadow and nervously
looking at the poles that she and Lauren
had laid out on the grass.

'Yes,' Lauren said, patting Twilight. 'Just
trot him over them.'

Mel turned Shadow towards the poles.
The little dapple-grey pony glanced once

at Twilight, and then trotted bravely over
them.

'He did it!' Mel exclaimed in
astonishment.

'I told you!' Lauren said. 'Now try
again.'

So Mel did. By the time Shadow had
trotted and cantered over the poles ten
times, Mel was beaming from ear to ear.
'Maybe I'll be able to get him to jump in
the end,' she said. She got off Shadow and
hugged him. 'You're such a good boy!'

Shadow snorted and Lauren was sure
that he looked pleased.

After untacking the ponies and turning
them out into Shadow's paddock to

graze, Lauren and Mel went up the path
to see Sparkle and her two kittens in the
barn.

Star and Midnight were awake. They
were toddling round the nest of hay, their
heads looking almost too large for their
fluffy black bodies.

'Which one's which?' Lauren asked.
They looked identical to her.

'Star's got a white star shape on her
tummy,' Mel explained. She picked up the
kitten nearest her. 'Look.'

'Oh, yes!' Lauren laughed, seeing the
white hairs.

'Do you want to hold her?' Mel asked.

Lauren nodded eagerly and Mel
handed Star over. The little kitten looked

into Lauren's face and then miaowed, her
mouth opening so wide that Lauren
could see all the way to the back of her
pink throat. 'Hello,' Lauren murmured.
'Aren't you lovely?' Star cuddled into her
arms.

'Wasn't Shadow good today?' Mel said to Lauren as she picked up Midnight.

'Yes, he was,' Lauren said. 'I'm sure he'll learn to jump in the end.'

'I hope so,' said Mel. 'I just wish he could learn in time for the meeting on Saturday. Jade and Monica are being so mean about him and the only thing that's going to stop them is if he learns to jump.' She looked at Lauren hopefully. 'Do you think we might have him jumping soon?'

'We might,' Lauren said. 'Fingers crossed.'

As Lauren rode Twilight home, she couldn't stop thinking about Mel's words.

Shadow might be able to learn to jump
with help, but how long would that take?
It might take ages and Mel would just
continue to get teased.

*If only we could teach him to jump more
quickly,* Lauren thought.

She remembered what Twilight had
said about his powers – he had some but
he didn't know what they were. Maybe
he did have some magic that could help.
But how could they find out?

And then the answer came to her. *Mrs
Fontana.* Mrs Fontana was the only other
person in the world who knew Twilight's
secret. She'd told Lauren that unicorns
existed and had given Lauren an old
book that contained the words of the

Turning Spell. If anyone would be able to help, she would.

As soon as she got home, Lauren ran into the house. Her mum was working on her computer.

'Mum,' Lauren said, 'can you take me to Mrs Fontana's bookshop?'

Mrs Foster frowned. 'Why?'

Lauren didn't know what to say. 'I . . . I want to ask Mrs Fontana something,' she said. 'It's for a project I'm doing. I thought Mrs Fontana might be able to help.'

'Well, actually I was going to go into town,' Mrs Foster said. 'I need to get some film for the camera. Max wants to

take some photos of Buddy to show to
his teacher. You could go and see Mrs
Fontana while I pick up the film.'

'Great!' Lauren said.

'Get changed then,' Mrs Foster said.
'We'll go right now.'

Almost before Mrs Foster had parked,
Lauren scrambled out of the car.

'I'll meet you there,' Mrs Foster said.
'Don't go anywhere else.'

'Don't worry, I won't,' Lauren
promised.

She raced over to the bookshop with
its brown and gold sign. A chime jangled
as she pushed open the door. There was
the familiar rose-patterned carpet on the

floor and the air smelled faintly of
blackcurrants. Books spilled off every
shelf and surface.

Walter, Mrs Fontana's terrier, came
trotting over as soon as Lauren walked
inside. 'Hi, boy,' Lauren said, bending
down to pat him. As she straightened up,
she saw that the old lady had appeared, as
if by magic. Mrs Fontana's face was lined
and wrinkled but her blue eyes shone
out, bright and clear. She had a mustard-
yellow shawl clasped loosely around her
shoulders and her long grey hair was
pinned up in a bun.

'Hello, Lauren,' she said. 'What can I
do for you today?'

Lauren hesitated. It was so hard to

launch straight into a discussion about
unicorns in broad daylight. 'Well . . . er . . .'

Mrs Fontana looked over her shoulder
to where a couple of people were
browsing along a bookshelf. 'Come down
to the children's section,' she said softly.
'Walter will tell me if I'm needed.'

The black and white terrier jumped
up on to the counter by the till and sat
down, his ears pricked. It was as if he'd
understood every word Mrs Fontana had
said.

Lauren followed Mrs Fontana to the
children's section at one side of the shop.
There was an armchair and cushions on
the floor. 'So how's Twilight?' Mrs
Fontana said, sitting down.

'Fine,' Lauren replied. She lowered her voice. 'We're trying to help this pony, Mrs Fontana. He belongs to my friend and he's scared of jumping.' She quickly explained about Shadow. 'He's so scared that it might take ages to get him jumping properly,' she said. 'Do you know if Twilight has any magical powers that could help?'

Mrs Fontana smiled. 'Twilight has many magical powers, Lauren. But I cannot tell you what they are. A unicorn has to discover his powers for himself.' She leaned forward and took Lauren's hands in hers. 'Don't worry, Twilight *is* able to help this pony,' she said. 'But it is up to you to help him work out how,

Lauren. You became a Unicorn Friend
because you have a good heart and the
imagination to believe in magic. Use
those qualities and together you and
Twilight will discover his powers.'

Letting go of Lauren's hands, she
straightened up. Her face looked less
serious now. 'So,' she said, her eyes
crinkling up at the corners in a smile,
'has Buddy found out Twilight's secret
yet?'

Lauren stared at her. How had Mrs
Fontana known about the problems she
was having with Buddy?

Mrs Fontana seemed to sense her
astonishment. 'When I was a Unicorn
Friend I had a dog who was very curious

about my unicorn,' she explained. 'He almost found my secret out several times.'

'You had your own unicorn?' Lauren gasped. She'd known that Mrs Fontana had seen a unicorn, but the old lady had never told her that she too had once been a Unicorn Friend.

'I did,' Mrs Fontana said softly. 'A long time ago.'

A hundred questions bubbled up inside Lauren. What had Mrs Fontana's unicorn been like? What had it been called? How had Mrs Fontana discovered that it was a unicorn? And, most of all, what had happened to it? Why didn't Mrs Fontana have it any more?

But before she could ask any of these questions, Walter barked.

'A customer must need help,' Mrs Fontana said, getting to her feet. She smiled at Lauren. 'Good luck with Shadow, Lauren. I hope you and Twilight can find a way to help, and be careful with Buddy. Try not to let him find out Twilight's secret.'

With that, Mrs Fontana went to the front of the shop where someone was waiting to pay for their books.

The shop door opened and Mrs Foster walked in. Lauren ran over. 'Hi, Mum.'

'Are you ready to go?' Mrs Foster asked.

Lauren nodded. 'Bye, Mrs Fontana,' she

said, glancing over to the desk where the old woman was wrapping up the customer's purchases.

Mrs Fontana looked up. 'Goodbye, Lauren,' she said. She smiled. 'And good luck.'

CHAPTER
Six

That evening, Lauren crept out of
the house again.

'Are we going to see Shadow?'
Twilight asked.

'Yes. Let's be quick,' Lauren said,
getting on to his back.

As they flew to Goose Creek Farm,
she told him what Mrs Fontana had
said. 'You have got powers that can

help,' she told him.

'But how can I use them if I don't know what they are?' Twilight said.

'I don't know,' Lauren admitted. She'd been thinking the same thing ever since she'd left Mrs Fontana's shop.

Shadow was waiting for them. He whinnied.

'You were great today, Shadow!' Twilight said as he landed.

Shadow bowed his head, as if a bit embarrassed by the praise. He snorted.

'He wants to know if he should have another go at trotting over the poles,' Twilight told Lauren.

'What about trying a small jump?' Lauren suggested hopefully.

Shadow looked worried.

'Go on, just have a go,' Twilight said.

Shadow hesitated for a moment and then slowly nodded his head.

Before Shadow could change his mind, Lauren scrambled off Twilight and put up a tiny jump. 'You can do it, Shadow!' she said.

Shadow nodded his head and, turning towards the jump, he began to trot.

'He's going to do it!' Lauren gasped to Twilight.

But then Shadow stopped dead.

'Oh dear,' Lauren sighed.

She and Twilight trotted over. Shadow was standing a few metres away from the jump. 'What went wrong?' Lauren asked him. 'Why did you stop?'

The dapple-grey pony hung his head and snorted sadly.

'He was just too scared,' Twilight told Lauren.

Shadow looked so dejected that Lauren
was sure that if ponies could cry, he
would have been in tears.

Twilight stepped forward and touched
his glowing horn to Shadow's neck. 'It's
OK,' Lauren heard him say softly. 'You
tried your best. Don't be upset.'

They stood there for a moment, and
then Lauren saw the little dapple-grey
pony's ears flicker forward. He raised his
head and whickered in a surprised sort of
way.

'What's he saying?' Lauren asked Twilight.

'That he's feeling a bit better,' Twilight
replied.

Shadow whickered again.

'Much better,' Twilight said.

Lauren saw Shadow look at the jump. His eyes suddenly seemed to be full of confidence. He whinnied.

'In fact, he says he feels so much better that he thinks he might be able to clear the jump,' Twilight said, looking astonished.

Shadow pricked up his ears and trotted away from them. Turning towards the jump, he started to canter. Lauren and Twilight watched in amazement as he flew over it.

'He jumped it!' Lauren exclaimed.

Shadow came cantering back to them, whinnying.

'He says that when we were talking he suddenly felt really brave,' Twilight said,

stamping his front hoof in excitement.
'He says he's never felt like that before,
but it was as if he just knew he could
do it.'

Shadow nuzzled Twilight and suddenly
Lauren's eyes widened. 'Your horn!' she
exclaimed to Twilight. 'You were

touching him with your horn when he
started to feel brave. Perhaps that's one of
your magical powers. Maybe by touching
him you gave him your courage – a
unicorn's bravery.'

Shadow tossed his head and whinnied.

'He says he doesn't care what
happened, he's just glad that he could do
it,' Twilight said.

Shadow nodded his head, and then he
turned and cantered over the jump again.

Lauren hugged Twilight in delight.
'This is brilliant!' she said. 'Mel is going
to be so pleased.' Her heart sang. She
couldn't wait to see her friend's face
when she jumped Shadow tomorrow!

★

Lauren was even more pleased by their night's work when Jade started teasing Mel again the next day at lunchtime.

'Still planning on going to the meeting on Saturday, are you, Mel?' Jade asked, coming over to them as they put their trays away. 'I don't know why you're bothering. It's not like Shadow will jump. Can't your parents afford to buy you a better pony?'

'Mel doesn't want another pony,' Lauren said, unable to bear their teasing a second longer. 'Shadow's fine.'

Jade laughed. 'Yeah, right,' she said, walking off laughing.

Lauren looked at her friend. Mel was biting her lip in frustration. 'I hate her!'

she burst out. 'I think I'm just going to tell Dad that I don't want to go on Saturday.'

'You can't,' Lauren said. 'You've got to come, Mel. If you don't, Jade and Monica will tease you again next week.' Mel looked even more miserable. 'Shadow will be good,' Lauren went on. 'In fact, when you ride him today I'm sure he's going to jump.'

Mel looked at her doubtfully. 'You think so?'

'I know so,' Lauren said confidently.

As soon as Lauren got home after school, she gave Twilight a quick brush over and rode him round to Mel's. 'I can't wait to see her face when Shadow jumps,' Lauren said to him, as they trotted along the road.

Mel was just putting Shadow's saddle on when they arrived. When they rode into the paddock, Lauren set up the jump exactly as she had done the night before.

Then she got back on Twilight. 'Try
Shadow now!' she called to Mel.

'OK,' Mel said. She turned Shadow
towards the jump. His ears pricked up
and he quickened his stride.

'He's going to jump it!' Lauren
whispered to Twilight in delight.

Shadow got nearer and nearer, his
hooves thudding on the grass.

Then, a metre in front of the jump, he
suddenly stopped.

CHAPTER

Seven

Lauren gasped in disappointment. After last night, she'd been sure that Shadow was going to jump the fence.

Twilight snorted and Lauren knew he was just as surprised as she was that Shadow had stopped.

Mel turned the dapple-grey pony away from the jump. 'I'll try him again,' she called. 'It almost felt like he was going to jump it then.' But when she tried again, Shadow wouldn't go anywhere near the fence.

Mel rode back to Lauren looking bitterly disappointed. 'I guess I should have known better than to think he would jump it,' she said. Shadow hung his head sadly. Mel hugged him. 'Don't worry, boy. I still love you.'

Despite her words, Shadow looked very upset. He didn't prick his ears up once, not even when they played catch.

'I think I'll take him in,' Mel said at last. 'He doesn't seem very happy.'

Lauren nodded. 'I'm sorry, Mel,' she said, as they dismounted.

'It's not your fault,' Mel said with a sigh.

Lauren didn't hang around for long.
She had a feeling that Mel wanted to be
on her own and so, after a bit, she got
back on to Twilight and rode him home.

'What went wrong?' she said to him.
'Why didn't Shadow jump?'

Twilight shook his head and snorted.

'I'll come down to your paddock
tonight,' Lauren told him. 'We've got to
sort this out.'

She was grooming Twilight back at
Granger's Farm when Buddy came
running down the path towards them. He
skidded to a stop and began to sniff
around Twilight's hooves.

'Buddy, go away!' Lauren said.

Buddy sat down and, cocking his head on one side, he whined at Twilight.

Just then, Max came running down the path. 'There you are, Buddy!' he said, as the puppy trotted over to meet him. Buddy licked his hand and then turned back to Twilight and woofed.

Max frowned. 'Why does Buddy act so weird around Twilight, Lauren?'

'I don't know,' Lauren said. 'Look, I'm trying to groom him. Why don't you take Buddy for a walk, Max?'

But Max didn't seem to be listening. Suddenly his eyes widened as he looked at Twilight. 'Maybe Twilight's an alien, Lauren!' he gasped.

'An alien!' Lauren stared at him.

'Yeah, maybe Twilight's an alien from another planet. He's in disguise so that he can spy on us and Buddy knows it.'

'Don't be dumb, Max. Twilight's just a pony,' Lauren said, desperately trying to act as if Max was totally crazy.

'So why does Buddy act so weird around him, then?' Max said.

'Because . . . because he's not used to horses,' Lauren said quickly.

But Max didn't look convinced. 'I'm going to tell Mum,' he said and, turning, he ran back up the path.

Lauren stared after him. She was sure her mum would just laugh at Max's idea about aliens, but the last thing she wanted was Max going on and on saying that there was something odd about Twilight.

'You see all the trouble you're causing?' she said to Buddy, who was sniffing at Twilight's tail.

CHAPTER

Eight

It was Lauren's turn to help wash the
dishes after supper. Once they were all
dried and put away, she pulled on her
boots. 'I'm going to see Twilight, Mum,'
she said.

'OK,' Mrs Foster said. She looked
round. 'Has anyone seen Max?'

Lauren and her dad shook their heads.
Mrs Foster smiled. 'He's probably in

his room drawing aliens.'

'Or Twilight's spaceship,' Mr Foster said
with a laugh.

Lauren let herself out of the back door,
feeling very relieved that her mum and
dad were treating her brother's suspicions
as a joke.

'Hi, boy,' she called, as Twilight
whinnied to her from the paddock gate.
'Do you know why Shadow wouldn't
jump today?' she asked Twilight as soon as
she had turned him into a unicorn.

'No,' Twilight replied.

'Let's go and see him,' Lauren said.
'There has to be a reason.'

Twilight flew to Shadow's field. The
little dapple-grey pony was standing

quietly, still looking very unhappy.

'Oh, Shadow,' Lauren said, sliding off Twilight's back and going over to him. 'What went wrong today? Why couldn't you jump?'

Shadow whinnied.

'Oh,' Twilight said. He turned to Lauren. 'Poor Shadow. He says he really wanted to, but he just didn't feel brave enough without the touch of my horn.'

Shadow neighed sadly.

Lauren didn't like to see Shadow looking so upset. 'I don't know what to do,' she told Shadow. 'You know Twilight can't be a unicorn when there are other people around.'

Shadow nodded.

He didn't try jumping again that evening. After all, they knew he *could* jump at night when Twilight was a unicorn – it was jumping in the day that was the problem.

Lauren sighed unhappily as she and

Twilight flew home. She really wished there was something they could do to help.

The next morning at school, Mel looked serious. 'I've decided that I'm not going to try and jump Shadow ever again,' she told Lauren. 'It just makes him so miserable and I'd rather get teased than make him unhappy.'

'What will you do about the meeting on Saturday?' Lauren asked.

'I'll have to say that I don't want to jump him.' Mel glanced across the classroom to where Jade and Monica were sitting. 'And I'll just have to put up with whatever those two say.'

Lauren squeezed her arm comfortingly. 'Take no notice of them.'

'Easier said than done,' Mel sighed. She forced a smile on her face. 'Will you still come over with Twilight this afternoon though? We could go for a trail ride.'

Lauren nodded. 'Sure,' she said.

When Lauren got to Goose Creek Farm that afternoon, Mel was already mounted on Shadow. 'We'd better get going,' Mel said. 'Mum thinks there might be a storm coming.'

Lauren looked up at the overcast sky. The air certainly had a heavy, stormy feel about it.

They rode up the path towards the

woods. Mr Cassidy was fixing a fence
near to the hay-barn. 'Don't go out too
far,' he called.

'We'll stay close to the farm,' Mel
promised. 'Come on, Lauren! Let's go.'

They urged Shadow and Twilight into
a trot.

'Let's go into the woods,' Mel said.
'There's a great trail there with a sandy
bit where we can have a canter.'

'OK,' Lauren said, shortening
Twilight's reins. His ears flickered back
and forth. 'Come on, boy,' she said
encouragingly.

A few minutes later, they entered the
woods. The tops of the tall trees met over
their heads like a green ceiling. Lauren

smiled to herself. What would Mel say if
she knew that Twilight had jumped over
those very treetops with Lauren on his
back?

'Here's the long canter,' Mel said. The
trail stretched out in front of them,
straight and inviting. 'Are you ready?'

Lauren nodded.

Mel leaned forward and gave Shadow
his head. The dapple-grey pony bounded
into a canter. Twilight hesitated for a
moment and then, when Lauren
squeezed his side, he followed.

The wind whipped against Lauren's
face as she leaned forward and urged
Twilight on. His hooves thudded down
on the sand and she could feel a broad

grin stretch across her face. This was as
good as flying!

At last, the trail began to narrow and
they slowed Twilight and Shadow to a
trot and then to a walk. Both ponies were
breathing hard from the canter, so Lauren
and Mel let them walk for a while.

Suddenly, they heard a deep, low
rumbling noise. The leaves on the branches
nearest to them seemed to shiver slightly.

'Thunder!' Mel said, looking at Lauren
in alarm. 'We'd better turn around.'

As they began to trot back along the
trail, they heard a pitter-pattering of rain
on the leafy canopy above them.

Mel nodded and Shadow and Twilight
began to canter along the path. Lauren

felt worried. Her parents had warned her lots of times about not being out in a thunderstorm.

As they reached the entrance to the woods, Lauren reined Twilight in. A jagged flash of lightning forked down, lighting up the darkened sky.

'Maybe we should stay here,' Mel stammered, looking frightened.

'No, it's really dangerous to stay near trees,' Lauren said. 'The lightning might strike one of them.' She looked down the path towards the house. 'If we gallop, we'll be back in a minute,' she said, looking at the lights shining invitingly out of the farmhouse's windows. 'Come on!'

She leaned forward and Twilight
plunged out from the trees.

'Come on, Twilight,' Lauren urged,
leaning low over his neck like a jockey.
Twilight's hooves pounded as he galloped
down the track, passing the hay-barn and
heading towards the barn with Shadow's
stall.

Suddenly, Lauren saw Mel's dad
standing in the barn's entrance.

Reaching Mr Cassidy, Twilight skidded
to a halt. Shadow was only a metre
behind.

'Quick!' Mr Cassidy shouted above the
noise of the storm. 'Get into the barn
before the rain gets any heavier!'

Lauren and Mel flung themselves off

Twilight and Shadow's backs and ran
with them inside.

'I've never seen a storm blow up so
quickly,' Mr Cassidy said.

Suddenly, there was a clap of thunder
and at the same time the sky outside lit
up with a bright white flash of lightning.
There was a loud bang nearby.

Mr Cassidy ran to the entrance and
looked out. 'A tree by the hay-barn's
been hit. It's on fire!' he exclaimed. 'I'm
going to have to call the fire department.
You stay here while I go to the house. I
don't want you outside in this.'

'But what about the fire?' Mel cried.

'It's all right. It won't reach you here,'
Mr Cassidy said. 'I'll be back as soon as I

can.' And with that, he ducked his head
and ran out.

Lauren led Twilight to the entrance
and looked up the track towards the hay-
barn. The tall oak tree that stood next to
it was burning brightly.

Mel joined her. 'If it falls, the whole
barn will go up in flames! Dad had better
be . . .' She broke off, her eyes widening.
'Sparkle!' she cried in horror. 'Lauren!
Sparkle and her kittens are inside!'

CHAPTER
Nine

Mel put her foot in the stirrup and swung herself up on to Shadow's back.

'What are you doing?' Lauren exclaimed.

'I've got to save Sparkle,' Mel said, digging her heels into Shadow's sides and heading out.

'It's too dangerous, Mel!' Lauren cried.

But it was too late. Mel was already

cantering Shadow up the track towards the barn.

Lauren didn't hesitate. Swinging herself up on Twilight's back, she galloped after her friend. 'Mel! Stop!' she yelled. She hated the thought of Sparkle and the kittens being trapped in the barn, but she knew Mel's life could be in danger if she went inside.

But Mel didn't listen. She urged Shadow past the burning tree and up to the barn door. Jumping off his back, she hauled it open.

Sparkle came racing out. She was carrying one of the kittens in her mouth. Lauren saw a flash of white on the kitten's tummy. Star! But what about

Midnight? He must still be inside.

To her horror, Lauren saw Mel loop Shadow's reins over her arm and run into the barn.

Twilight gave an alarmed whinny. There was a loud creak. Lauren looked up. A huge burning branch of the oak tree looked as if it was about to break off.

'Mel!' she shouted. 'Get out!'

Mel appeared on foot in the doorway of the barn, clutching Midnight.

'Quick!' Lauren yelled, looking up at the tree.

But it was too late. Before Mel could get out of the barn, there was a loud crack and the burning branch crashed to the ground in front of the barn door.

Mel screamed and Lauren gasped. The branch was blocking the way out!

Lauren could just see Mel's terrified

eyes through the smoke that was filling the air. There was only one way for her to get out.

'Get up on Shadow and make him jump the branch, Mel!' Lauren cried. 'It's the only way.'

'But he won't do it!' Mel shouted.

'Just try!' Lauren called.

Clutching Midnight to her chest, Mel scrambled on to Shadow's back.

Lauren glanced around, desperately hoping to see Mr Cassidy or the fire department arriving, but there was no one there. 'Shadow, please!' she yelled, as Mel began to trot him towards the log. 'You've got to jump it! For Mel!'

She heard Shadow neigh uncertainly

through the smoke. *Please jump it,* Lauren prayed. *You might not have Twilight's magical powers to help you, but you can still do it. Please, Shadow, please!*

She saw Shadow hesitate and dread gripped her heart. He wasn't going to be able to do it.

'Melanie!' Hearing a hoarse cry, Lauren swung round. Mr Cassidy was running up the hill towards them, looking horrified. For a moment, Lauren felt a surge of hope but then her heart plummeted. It was obvious that Mr Cassidy couldn't move the log on his own. There was still only one way for Mel to get out and that was for Shadow to jump.

Twilight seemed to realize the same

thing. Throwing his head back, he whinnied loudly to Shadow. As he did so, a fork of lightning flashed across the sky, making every hair of his grey body shine with a bright white light.

Suddenly, Lauren saw a new look of bravery flash into Shadow's eyes. Tossing his head back, just like Twilight, he broke into a canter. Mel grabbed hold of his mane with her free hand. Shadow's stride lengthened. His ears pricked and the next second, he was soaring over the burning log, clearing it with ease.

Mel was hanging on to Midnight, a look of astonishment, relief and delight on her face as they galloped up to Twilight. 'He did it!' she said, sliding off

Shadow's back as he halted. 'He jumped it, Lauren! He actually jumped it.'

'He was amazing!' Lauren cried, and

Twilight whinnied in agreement.

Just then Mr Cassidy reached them.
'Mel! Oh my goodness,' he said, his
breath coming in short gasps. 'I thought
you weren't going to get out. What were
you doing in the hay-barn?'

'Rescuing Midnight,' Mel stammered.

'But I told you not to leave the barn,'
Mr Cassidy said, pulling her into his arms
and kissing her. 'I'm just so glad you're
safe.'

'And it's all because of Shadow,' Mel
said, breaking free and hugging the
dapple-grey pony. 'Wasn't he wonderful,
Dad?'

Mr Cassidy smiled at Shadow. 'The
best.'

Shadow whickered proudly, happiness lighting up his dark eyes.

As the fire crew arrived and began to put out the fire, Mr Cassidy helped the girls make up a special feed of warm bran, carrots and molasses for Shadow and Twilight. Once the two ponies were dry and bedded down in two stalls, Lauren and Mel went inside.

'I can hardly move I feel so tired,' Mel said, as she and Lauren kicked off their boots by the back door.

'Me too,' Lauren agreed.

Mrs Cassidy was waiting for them. She was upset with Mel for taking such a risk but she was so relieved that both girls were safe that she made them enormous mugs of hot chocolate with marshmallows floating on top.

As Lauren looked out of the kitchen to where the fire crew was saying goodbye to Mr Cassidy, she breathed a sigh of relief. Luckily the flames hadn't spread to the barn, so Mr Cassidy's hay was OK.

In fact, Lauren thought, *everything has turned out OK.* She and Mel and both horses were safe. Midnight, the kitten, had been reunited with Sparkle and Mel had made the little family a new bed in the stall next to Shadow.

Lauren shivered as she realized that it could have all been so different. If it hadn't been for Shadow's bravery, she

didn't like to think what might have
happened. She remembered the way he
had hesitated as he'd approached the log.
How had he suddenly found the courage
that he needed to jump it?

That night, when Lauren turned
Twilight into a unicorn, she asked him if
he knew how Shadow had found the
courage to jump.

'No, I don't,' Twilight admitted. 'Shall
we go and visit him to find out?'

Lauren mounted and, with a kick of
Twilight's back legs, they rose into the
night sky.

Shadow was grazing near the bottom
of his moonlit paddock. Lauren jumped

off Twilight's back and ran over to him.
'You were amazing today, Shadow,' she
said, as he whinnied a greeting. 'I didn't
think you were going to do it but you
were so brave. What made you able to
jump?'

Shadow neighed.

'He says that when the lightning
flashed it made me look like a unicorn,'
Twilight translated for Lauren. 'He
realized that if he was going to save Mel,
he had to be as brave as he was the other
night when my horn touched him – as
brave as a unicorn.'

Lauren nodded, remembering the look
that had come into Shadow's eyes as the
lightning had shone on Twilight's coat. It

all made sense. She looked at the dapple-grey pony. 'Well, you were wonderful, Shadow, and, best of all, now that you've jumped that great big log, the jumps at Pony Club will seem tiny. You'll be able to jump them easily.'

Shadow snorted doubtfully.

'He doesn't think so,' Twilight interpreted. 'He says that he could only jump the log because he had to.'

Lauren frowned. 'But Twilight wasn't a unicorn when you jumped that log, Shadow. You jumped that log because you were brave.'

Twilight whickered in agreement.

Shadow stared at Lauren as if she'd said something totally astonishing.

'You saved Mel's life, Shadow,' Lauren said softly. 'If you can do that, you can do anything.'

A new look of confidence began to shine in Shadow's eyes.

Lauren climbed on to Twilight's back. 'We'd better go,' she said. 'Goodnight, Shadow.'

Shadow whinnied proudly and tossed his mane as Lauren rode Twilight off into the night.

On Saturday afternoon, Lauren stood beside Twilight, watching Mel ride Shadow towards the first jump in the course that Kathy, their Pony Club trainer, had set out.

It had taken a lot for Lauren to
persuade Mel to have a go at the
jumping course but, after being reminded
of Shadow's huge leap over the burning
log, she had finally agreed.

'I don't know why Mel's bothering.'
Jade's snide voice cut through the air. She
was watching with Monica. 'Shadow's
never going to jump a course of jumps –
last month he wouldn't even jump one.'

Lauren didn't say anything. She just
crossed her fingers. The course was small
but twisty and no one in the group had
managed a clear round yet.

Jade's pony, Prince, had knocked three
fences over and Monica's pony, Scout, had
had three refusals. Twilight had only had

one fence down, which Lauren didn't
mind at all because she knew he'd tried
his best. She crossed her fingers as Mel
cantered Shadow towards the first jump.

She held her breath. Would Shadow
stop?

But, to her delight, the dapple-grey
pony's ears pricked up, his stride
lengthened and he jumped perfectly over
the fence. He cantered to the next one
and then the next. As he cleared the last
fence, everyone burst into applause for a
perfect clear round.

Mel patted Shadow as if she was never
going to stop.

Seeing the happiness on Mel's and
Shadow's faces, Lauren hugged Twilight

in delight. 'Oh, Twilight, isn't it brilliant?' she whispered. 'I'm so glad you were able to help.'

Twilight shook his head and pushed his nose against her chest.

Lauren understood him perfectly. 'OK then,' she said, putting her arm round his neck. 'I'm so glad *we* were able to help!'

My Secret Unicorn

When Lauren recites a secret spell, her pony
Twilight turns into a beautiful unicorn with magical
powers! Together Lauren and Twilight learn how to
use their magic to help their friends.

The Magic Spell
Linda Chapman

Dreams Come True
Linda Chapman

Flying High
Linda Chapman

Starlight Surprise
Linda Chapman

Stronger Than Magic
Linda Chapman

Look out for more **My Secret Unicorn** adventures